ONCE IN THE YEAR

BOOKS BY ELIZABETH YATES

Published by UPPER ROOM BOOKS

A Book of Hours

Up the Golden Stair

ONCE in the YEAR

A Christmas Story by
ELIZABETH YATES

Illustrated by
NORA S. UNWIN

UPPER ROOM BOOKS • Nashville

Once in the Year

Cover Illustration: Nora S. Unwin
Cover Design: Jim Bateman
First Upper Room Printing: September 1991 (10)
Second Upper Room Printing: July 1992 (5)
ISBN 0-8358-0626-X

Printed in the United States of America

MARTHA was making Christmas cookies and Peter sat on the stool in the kitchen watching her. The dough that had been chilled was rolled out very thin and then the deft hands cut it into shapes. The cookie cutter was one used only at this time of the year and its shape was that of a small fir tree. Martha brushed the cookies with egg white, sprinkled them with sugar and a pinch of ground nuts, then she ranged them on tins and put them in the oven. They were so thin that they were soon done and the good smell of their baking filled the kitchen.

Peter was hoping that one would break or crack so it might be given him to eat, but it was not until the last tin had come from the oven that Martha found a cookie for him. He took it and ate it slowly as a very special treat, a tiny bit of Christmas to have before Christmas actually came.

When the cookies were all laid out on trays to cool and Martha had washed the dishes and put them away, she took Peter's hand in hers and together they went in to the sitting room to light the Christmas candle and place it in the window. Twilight was coming down early on that short December day and the room was filled with gloom, waiting for the light of the candle.

"It must always be the first light in the

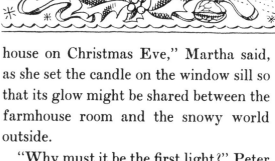

house on Christmas Eve," Martha said, as she set the candle on the window sill so that its glow might be shared between the farmhouse room and the snowy world outside.

"Why must it be the first light?" Peter asked.

Martha shook her head slowly. "My mother told me that it must be when I was no bigger than you are now, and her mother told her the same when she was a little girl. It's a Christmas custom, like so many of the things we do at this time of year, grown no one knows quite how or where but rooted deep in the heart's kindness."

Martha and Peter stood by the window watching the light flicker and gain

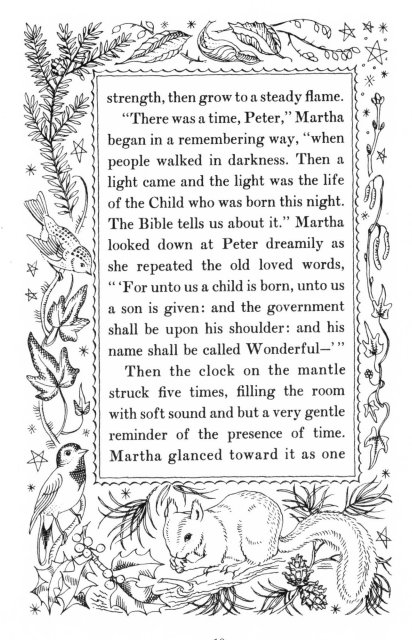

strength, then grow to a steady flame.

"There was a time, Peter," Martha began in a remembering way, "when people walked in darkness. Then a light came and the light was the life of the Child who was born this night. The Bible tells us about it." Martha looked down at Peter dreamily as she repeated the old loved words, "'For unto us a child is born, unto us a son is given: and the government shall be upon his shoulder: and his name shall be called Wonderful—'"

Then the clock on the mantle struck five times, filling the room with soft sound and but a very gentle reminder of the presence of time. Martha glanced toward it as one

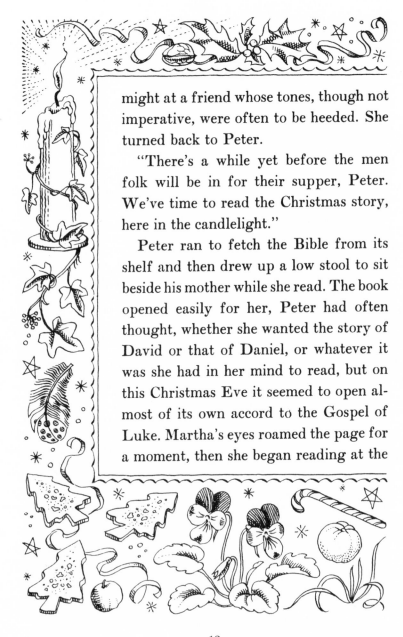

might at a friend whose tones, though not imperative, were often to be heeded. She turned back to Peter.

"There's a while yet before the men folk will be in for their supper, Peter. We've time to read the Christmas story, here in the candlelight."

Peter ran to fetch the Bible from its shelf and then drew up a low stool to sit beside his mother while she read. The book opened easily for her, Peter had often thought, whether she wanted the story of David or that of Daniel, or whatever it was she had in her mind to read, but on this Christmas Eve it seemed to open almost of its own accord to the Gospel of Luke. Martha's eyes roamed the page for a moment, then she began reading at the

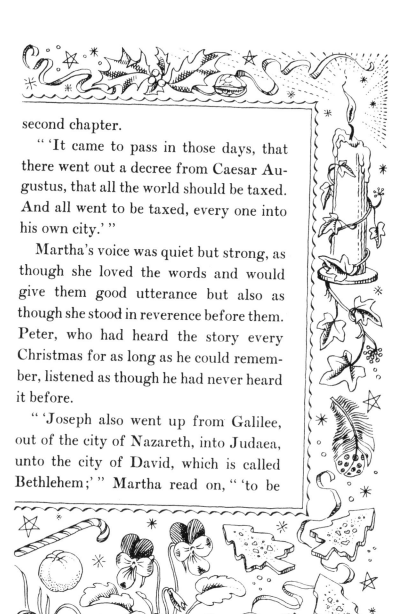

second chapter.

"'It came to pass in those days, that there went out a decree from Caesar Augustus, that all the world should be taxed. And all went to be taxed, every one into his own city.'"

Martha's voice was quiet but strong, as though she loved the words and would give them good utterance but also as though she stood in reverence before them. Peter, who had heard the story every Christmas for as long as he could remember, listened as though he had never heard it before.

"'Joseph also went up from Galilee, out of the city of Nazareth, into Judaea, unto the city of David, which is called Bethlehem;'" Martha read on, "'to be

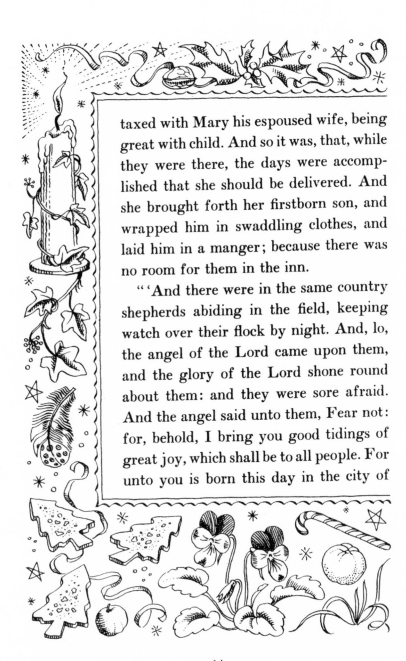

taxed with Mary his espoused wife, being great with child. And so it was, that, while they were there, the days were accomplished that she should be delivered. And she brought forth her firstborn son, and wrapped him in swaddling clothes, and laid him in a manger; because there was no room for them in the inn.

" 'And there were in the same country shepherds abiding in the field, keeping watch over their flock by night. And, lo, the angel of the Lord came upon them, and the glory of the Lord shone round about them: and they were sore afraid. And the angel said unto them, Fear not: for, behold, I bring you good tidings of great joy, which shall be to all people. For unto you is born this day in the city of

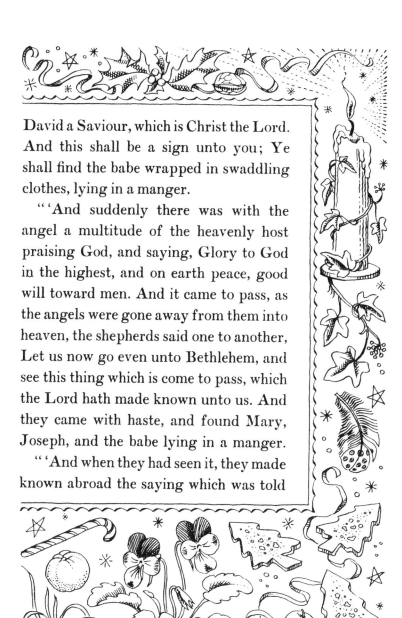

David a Saviour, which is Christ the Lord. And this shall be a sign unto you; Ye shall find the babe wrapped in swaddling clothes, lying in a manger.

" 'And suddenly there was with the angel a multitude of the heavenly host praising God, and saying, Glory to God in the highest, and on earth peace, good will toward men. And it came to pass, as the angels were gone away from them into heaven, the shepherds said one to another, Let us now go even unto Bethlehem, and see this thing which is come to pass, which the Lord hath made known unto us. And they came with haste, and found Mary, Joseph, and the babe lying in a manger.

" 'And when they had seen it, they made known abroad the saying which was told

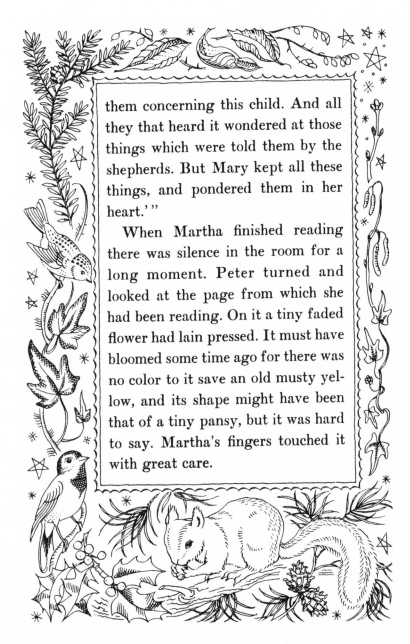

them concerning this child. And all they that heard it wondered at those things which were told them by the shepherds. But Mary kept all these things, and pondered them in her heart.' "

When Martha finished reading there was silence in the room for a long moment. Peter turned and looked at the page from which she had been reading. On it a tiny faded flower had lain pressed. It must have bloomed some time ago for there was no color to it save an old musty yellow, and its shape might have been that of a tiny pansy, but it was hard to say. Martha's fingers touched it with great care.

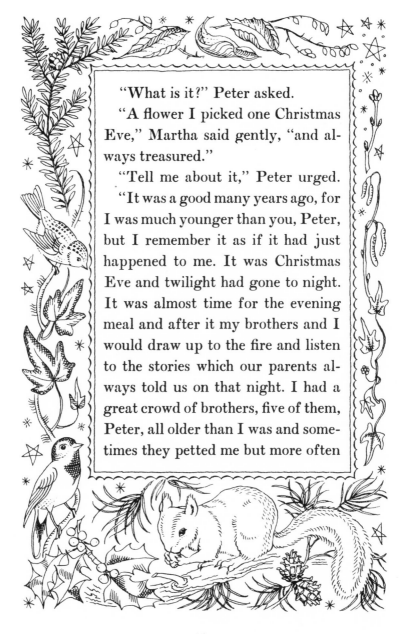

"What is it?" Peter asked.

"A flower I picked one Christmas Eve," Martha said gently, "and always treasured."

"Tell me about it," Peter urged.

"It was a good many years ago, for I was much younger than you, Peter, but I remember it as if it had just happened to me. It was Christmas Eve and twilight had gone to night. It was almost time for the evening meal and after it my brothers and I would draw up to the fire and listen to the stories which our parents always told us on that night. I had a great crowd of brothers, five of them, Peter, all older than I was and sometimes they petted me but more often

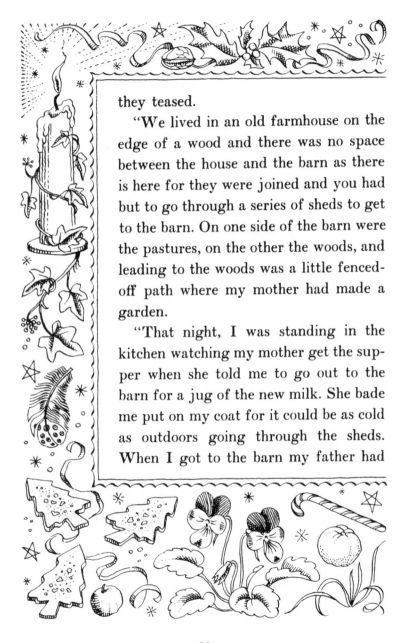

they teased.

"We lived in an old farmhouse on the edge of a wood and there was no space between the house and the barn as there is here for they were joined and you had but to go through a series of sheds to get to the barn. On one side of the barn were the pastures, on the other the woods, and leading to the woods was a little fenced-off path where my mother had made a garden.

"That night, I was standing in the kitchen watching my mother get the supper when she told me to go out to the barn for a jug of the new milk. She bade me put on my coat for it could be as cold as outdoors going through the sheds. When I got to the barn my father had

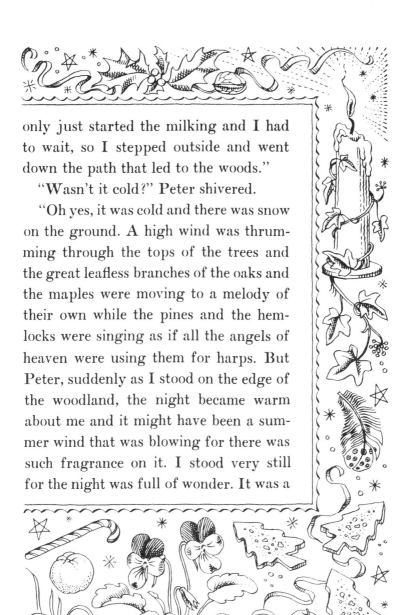

only just started the milking and I had to wait, so I stepped outside and went down the path that led to the woods."

"Wasn't it cold?" Peter shivered.

"Oh yes, it was cold and there was snow on the ground. A high wind was thrumming through the tops of the trees and the great leafless branches of the oaks and the maples were moving to a melody of their own while the pines and the hemlocks were singing as if all the angels of heaven were using them for harps. But Peter, suddenly as I stood on the edge of the woodland, the night became warm about me and it might have been a summer wind that was blowing for there was such fragrance on it. I stood very still for the night was full of wonder. It was a

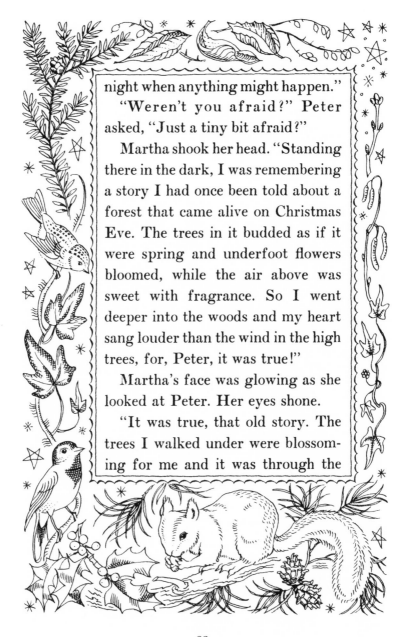

night when anything might happen."

"Weren't you afraid?" Peter asked, "Just a tiny bit afraid?"

Martha shook her head. "Standing there in the dark, I was remembering a story I had once been told about a forest that came alive on Christmas Eve. The trees in it budded as if it were spring and underfoot flowers bloomed, while the air above was sweet with fragrance. So I went deeper into the woods and my heart sang louder than the wind in the high trees, for, Peter, it was true!"

Martha's face was glowing as she looked at Peter. Her eyes shone.

"It was true, that old story. The trees I walked under were blossoming for me and it was through the

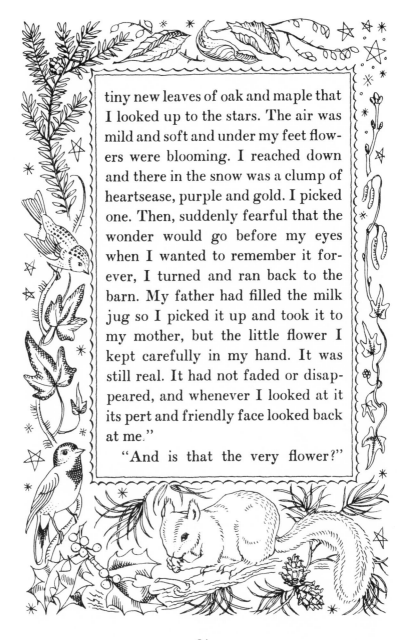

tiny new leaves of oak and maple that I looked up to the stars. The air was mild and soft and under my feet flowers were blooming. I reached down and there in the snow was a clump of heartsease, purple and gold. I picked one. Then, suddenly fearful that the wonder would go before my eyes when I wanted to remember it forever, I turned and ran back to the barn. My father had filled the milk jug so I picked it up and took it to my mother, but the little flower I kept carefully in my hand. It was still real. It had not faded or disappeared, and whenever I looked at it its pert and friendly face looked back at me."

"And is that the very flower?"

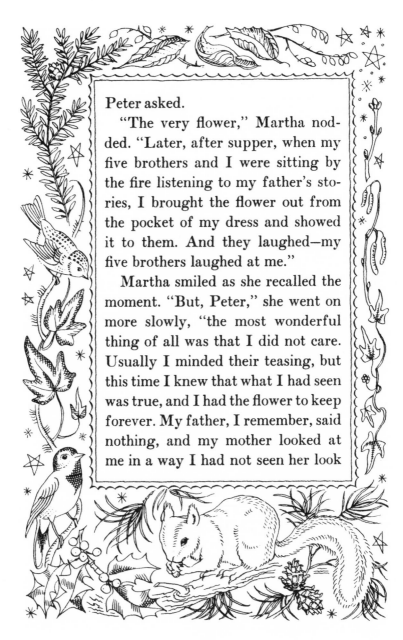

Peter asked.

"The very flower," Martha nodded. "Later, after supper, when my
five brothers and I were sitting by
the fire listening to my father's stories, I brought the flower out from
the pocket of my dress and showed
it to them. And they laughed—my
five brothers laughed at me."

Martha smiled as she recalled the
moment. "But, Peter," she went on
more slowly, "the most wonderful
thing of all was that I did not care.
Usually I minded their teasing, but
this time I knew that what I had seen
was true, and I had the flower to keep
forever. My father, I remember, said
nothing, and my mother looked at
me in a way I had not seen her look

26

before—equally, as if we shared the same life.

"Late that night, when she tucked me into bed, she told me that when something wonderful happened to people on Christmas Eve it was to be cherished in the heart and in the mind. She said that we must not be afraid of the wonderful things, nor must we let others laugh them away from us. Only thus do we learn to hold our dreams in the face of the world's derision."

"Nothing wonderful has ever happened to me on Christmas Eve," Peter said.

"Oh, but it will, Peter, it will, if your eyes are open and your heart is kind. I've not seen that flowering forest again but I know that it is there. On Christmas Eve

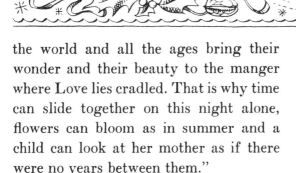

the world and all the ages bring their
wonder and their beauty to the manger
where Love lies cradled. That is why time
can slide together on this night alone,
flowers can bloom as in summer and a
child can look at her mother as if there
were no years between them."

The clock on the mantle raised its voice
—only one stroke, the half hour, but this
time it had meaning for Martha. She
closed the Bible, with the little faded
flower still pressed safely between the
pages of the Christmas story, and put the
book back on its shelf.

"It will soon be time for supper, Peter,"
she said, as she lit the lamps and busied
herself about the room.

Peter nodded. He was watching his
father and Benj come over the snow to

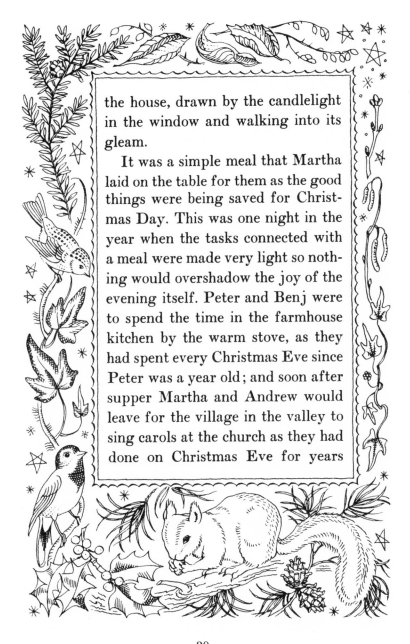

the house, drawn by the candlelight in the window and walking into its gleam.

It was a simple meal that Martha laid on the table for them as the good things were being saved for Christmas Day. This was one night in the year when the tasks connected with a meal were made very light so nothing would overshadow the joy of the evening itself. Peter and Benj were to spend the time in the farmhouse kitchen by the warm stove, as they had spent every Christmas Eve since Peter was a year old; and soon after supper Martha and Andrew would leave for the village in the valley to sing carols at the church as they had done on Christmas Eve for years

past. Peter never knew quite what time they got back to the farmhouse for it was always after he had gone to sleep.

When supper was over, Martha and Andrew put on their warm coats. Andrew pulled his cap down over his ears and Martha threw a woolen shawl over her head and tied it under her chin. Laughter was in their voices and lightness in their movements, for this was one time when care could be set aside. The animals had been fed early and bedded down for the night so that Andrew had no worries for them; and Martha had spent the whole week cooking and cleaning so her mind was free from household chores. Her husband and her son, and

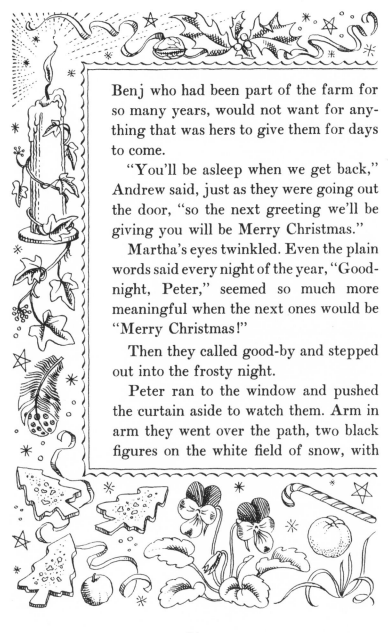

Benj who had been part of the farm for
so many years, would not want for anything that was hers to give them for days
to come.

"You'll be asleep when we get back,"
Andrew said, just as they were going out
the door, "so the next greeting we'll be
giving you will be Merry Christmas."

Martha's eyes twinkled. Even the plain
words said every night of the year, "Good-
night, Peter," seemed so much more
meaningful when the next ones would be
"Merry Christmas!"

Then they called good-by and stepped
out into the frosty night.

Peter ran to the window and pushed
the curtain aside to watch them. Arm in
arm they went over the path, two black
figures on the white field of snow, with

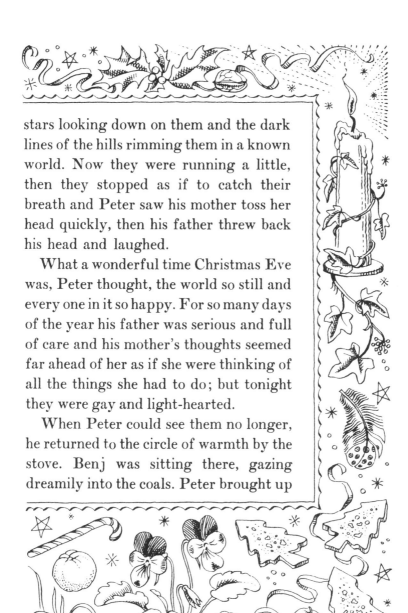

stars looking down on them and the dark lines of the hills rimming them in a known world. Now they were running a little, then they stopped as if to catch their breath and Peter saw his mother toss her head quickly, then his father threw back his head and laughed.

What a wonderful time Christmas Eve was, Peter thought, the world so still and every one in it so happy. For so many days of the year his father was serious and full of care and his mother's thoughts seemed far ahead of her as if she were thinking of all the things she had to do; but tonight they were gay and light-hearted.

When Peter could see them no longer, he returned to the circle of warmth by the stove. Benj was sitting there, gazing dreamily into the coals. Peter brought up

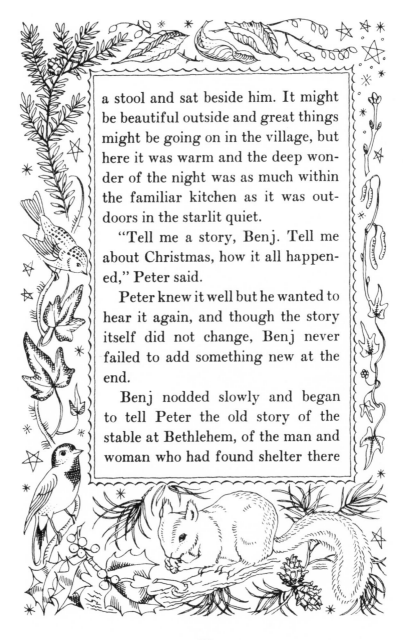

a stool and sat beside him. It might
be beautiful outside and great things
might be going on in the village, but
here it was warm and the deep wonder of the night was as much within
the familiar kitchen as it was outdoors in the starlit quiet.

"Tell me a story, Benj. Tell me
about Christmas, how it all happened," Peter said.

Peter knew it well but he wanted to
hear it again, and though the story
itself did not change, Benj never
failed to add something new at the
end.

Benj nodded slowly and began
to tell Peter the old story of the
stable at Bethlehem, of the man and
woman who had found shelter there

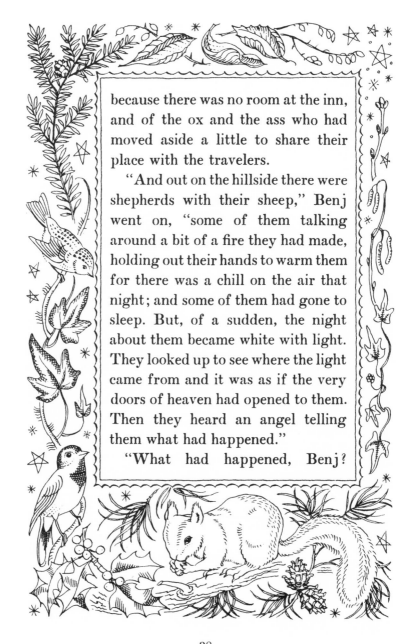

because there was no room at the inn, and of the ox and the ass who had moved aside a little to share their place with the travelers.

"And out on the hillside there were shepherds with their sheep," Benj went on, "some of them talking around a bit of a fire they had made, holding out their hands to warm them for there was a chill on the air that night; and some of them had gone to sleep. But, of a sudden, the night about them became white with light. They looked up to see where the light came from and it was as if the very doors of heaven had opened to them. Then they heard an angel telling them what had happened."

"What had happened, Benj?

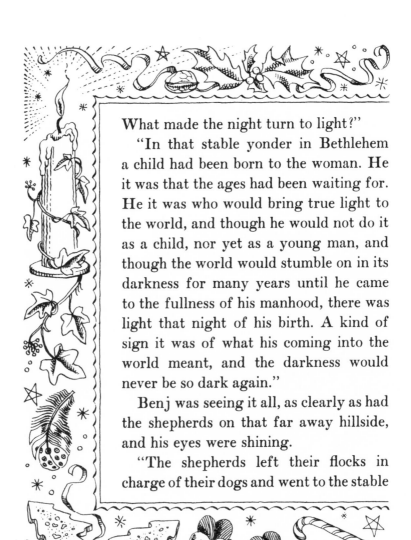

What made the night turn to light?"

"In that stable yonder in Bethlehem a child had been born to the woman. He it was that the ages had been waiting for. He it was who would bring true light to the world, and though he would not do it as a child, nor yet as a young man, and though the world would stumble on in its darkness for many years until he came to the fullness of his manhood, there was light that night of his birth. A kind of sign it was of what his coming into the world meant, and the darkness would never be so dark again."

Benj was seeing it all, as clearly as had the shepherds on that far away hillside, and his eyes were shining.

"The shepherds left their flocks in charge of their dogs and went to the stable

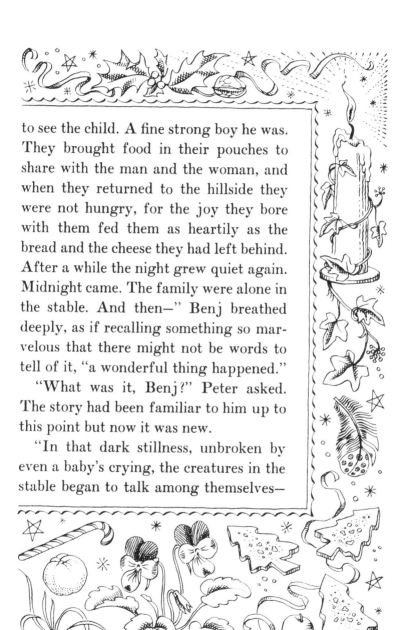

to see the child. A fine strong boy he was. They brought food in their pouches to share with the man and the woman, and when they returned to the hillside they were not hungry, for the joy they bore with them fed them as heartily as the bread and the cheese they had left behind. After a while the night grew quiet again. Midnight came. The family were alone in the stable. And then—" Benj breathed deeply, as if recalling something so marvelous that there might not be words to tell of it, "a wonderful thing happened."

"What was it, Benj?" Peter asked. The story had been familiar to him up to this point but now it was new.

"In that dark stillness, unbroken by even a baby's crying, the creatures in the stable began to talk among themselves—

41

the great slow-moving ox, and the tired little ass, a half-grown sheep that had followed the shepherds to Bethlehem, and a brown hen who had roosted in the rafters at sundown. They talked together and to the child."

"Didn't they talk to the others—the man and the woman?"

Benj shook his head. "Those two had gone to sleep." He looked at Peter and spoke slowly. "It's said that on every Christmas Eve, near midnight and for a while after, the creatures talk among themselves. It is the only time they do so, the only time of all the year."

"Can any one hear them, Benj?"

The old man shook his head again. "Only the still of heart, for only they will listen long enough to catch the mean-

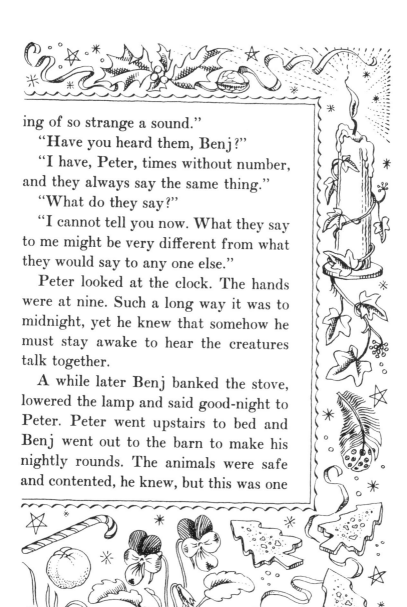

ing of so strange a sound."

"Have you heard them, Benj?"

"I have, Peter, times without number, and they always say the same thing."

"What do they say?"

"I cannot tell you now. What they say to me might be very different from what they would say to any one else."

Peter looked at the clock. The hands were at nine. Such a long way it was to midnight, yet he knew that somehow he must stay awake to hear the creatures talk together.

A while later Benj banked the stove, lowered the lamp and said good-night to Peter. Peter went upstairs to bed and Benj went out to the barn to make his nightly rounds. The animals were safe and contented, he knew, but this was one

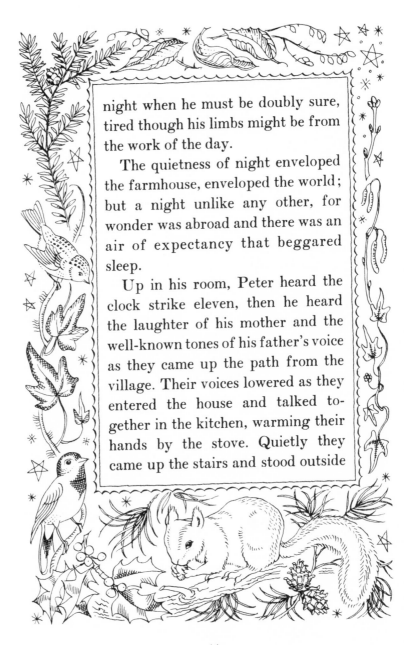

night when he must be doubly sure, tired though his limbs might be from the work of the day.

The quietness of night enveloped the farmhouse, enveloped the world; but a night unlike any other, for wonder was abroad and there was an air of expectancy that beggared sleep.

Up in his room, Peter heard the clock strike eleven, then he heard the laughter of his mother and the well-known tones of his father's voice as they came up the path from the village. Their voices lowered as they entered the house and talked together in the kitchen, warming their hands by the stove. Quietly they came up the stairs and stood outside

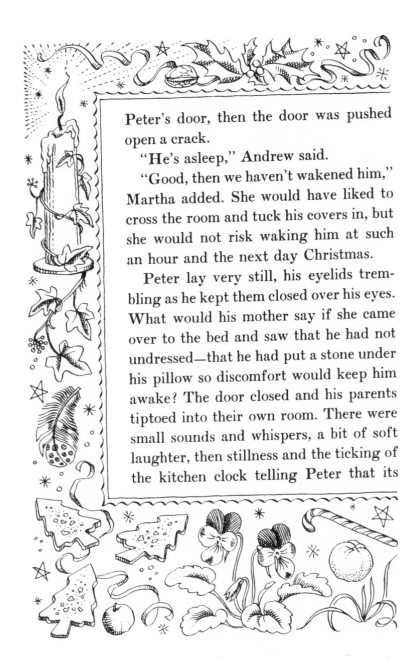

Peter's door, then the door was pushed open a crack.

"He's asleep," Andrew said.

"Good, then we haven't wakened him," Martha added. She would have liked to cross the room and tuck his covers in, but she would not risk waking him at such an hour and the next day Christmas.

Peter lay very still, his eyelids trembling as he kept them closed over his eyes. What would his mother say if she came over to the bed and saw that he had not undressed—that he had put a stone under his pillow so discomfort would keep him awake? The door closed and his parents tiptoed into their own room. There were small sounds and whispers, a bit of soft laughter, then stillness and the ticking of the kitchen clock telling Peter that its hands were drawing near midnight.

Slowly, one foot then another, he got out of bed and put on his coat that had been made from the wool of Biddy's last shearing. He took his shoes in his hands and crept down the stairs to the kitchen. Peering up into the face of the clock he saw the hands at a quarter to twelve. He sat down on the floor to put on his shoes. Going to the door he opened it noiselessly and closed it behind him, then ran lightly to the barn.

It was very still in the barn and very dark, but as his eyes became used to the darkness he could discern dimly the familiar shapes of the farm animals in their chosen positions of sleep. The barn seemed strange so near the mid hour of night and Peter, to assure himself, went to each

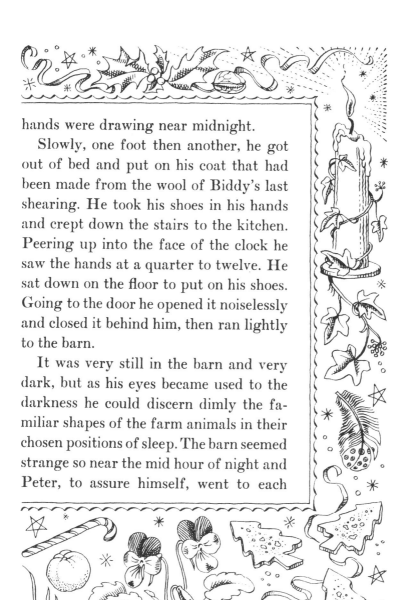

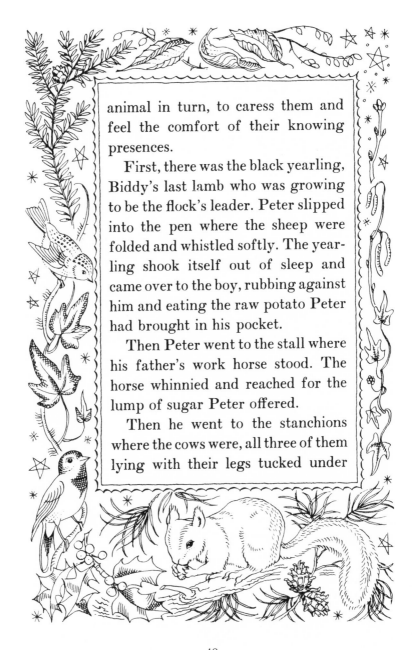

animal in turn, to caress them and feel the comfort of their knowing presences.

First, there was the black yearling, Biddy's last lamb who was growing to be the flock's leader. Peter slipped into the pen where the sheep were folded and whistled softly. The yearling shook itself out of sleep and came over to the boy, rubbing against him and eating the raw potato Peter had brought in his pocket.

Then Peter went to the stall where his father's work horse stood. The horse whinnied and reached for the lump of sugar Peter offered.

Then he went to the stanchions where the cows were, all three of them lying with their legs tucked under

48

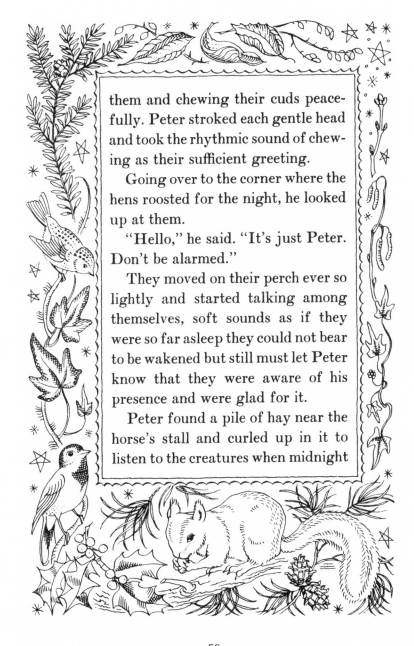

them and chewing their cuds peace-
fully. Peter stroked each gentle head
and took the rhythmic sound of chewing as their sufficient greeting.

Going over to the corner where the
hens roosted for the night, he looked
up at them.

"Hello," he said. "It's just Peter.
Don't be alarmed."

They moved on their perch ever so
lightly and started talking among
themselves, soft sounds as if they
were so far asleep they could not bear
to be wakened but still must let Peter
know that they were aware of his
presence and were glad for it.

Peter found a pile of hay near the
horse's stall and curled up in it to
listen to the creatures when midnight

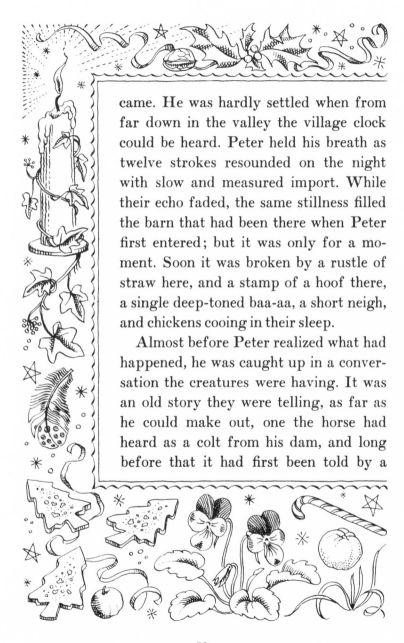

came. He was hardly settled when from far down in the valley the village clock could be heard. Peter held his breath as twelve strokes resounded on the night with slow and measured import. While their echo faded, the same stillness filled the barn that had been there when Peter first entered; but it was only for a moment. Soon it was broken by a rustle of straw here, and a stamp of a hoof there, a single deep-toned baa-aa, a short neigh, and chickens cooing in their sleep.

Almost before Peter realized what had happened, he was caught up in a conversation the creatures were having. It was an old story they were telling, as far as he could make out, one the horse had heard as a colt from his dam, and long before that it had first been told by a

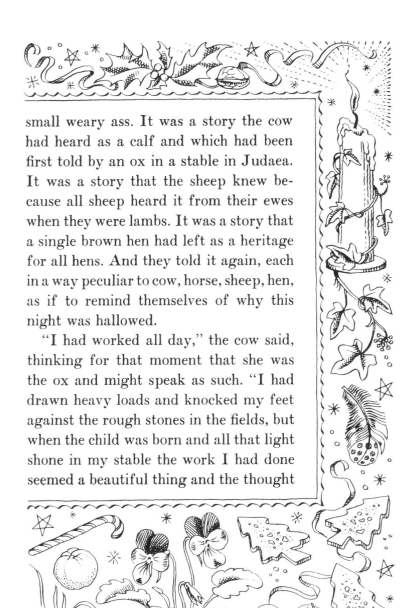

small weary ass. It was a story the cow had heard as a calf and which had been first told by an ox in a stable in Judaea. It was a story that the sheep knew because all sheep heard it from their ewes when they were lambs. It was a story that a single brown hen had left as a heritage for all hens. And they told it again, each in a way peculiar to cow, horse, sheep, hen, as if to remind themselves of why this night was hallowed.

"I had worked all day," the cow said, thinking for that moment that she was the ox and might speak as such. "I had drawn heavy loads and knocked my feet against the rough stones in the fields, but when the child was born and all that light shone in my stable the work I had done seemed a beautiful thing and the thought

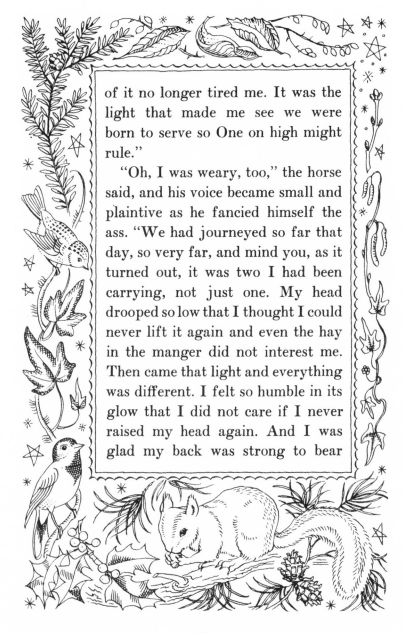

of it no longer tired me. It was the
light that made me see we were
born to serve so One on high might
rule."

"Oh, I was weary, too," the horse
said, and his voice became small and
plaintive as he fancied himself the
ass. "We had journeyed so far that
day, so very far, and mind you, as it
turned out, it was two I had been
carrying, not just one. My head
drooped so low that I thought I could
never lift it again and even the hay
in the manger did not interest me.
Then came that light and everything
was different. I felt so humble in its
glow that I did not care if I never
raised my head again. And I was
glad my back was strong to bear

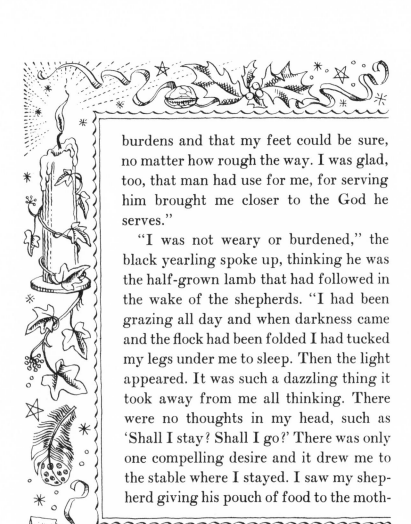

burdens and that my feet could be sure, no matter how rough the way. I was glad, too, that man had use for me, for serving him brought me closer to the God he serves."

"I was not weary or burdened," the black yearling spoke up, thinking he was the half-grown lamb that had followed in the wake of the shepherds. "I had been grazing all day and when darkness came and the flock had been folded I had tucked my legs under me to sleep. Then the light appeared. It was such a dazzling thing it took away from me all thinking. There were no thoughts in my head, such as 'Shall I stay? Shall I go?' There was only one compelling desire and it drew me to the stable where I stayed. I saw my shepherd giving his pouch of food to the moth-

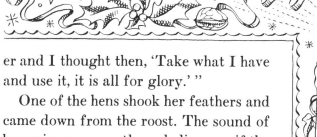

er and I thought then, 'Take what I have and use it, it is all for glory.' "

One of the hens shook her feathers and came down from the roost. The sound of her voice was sweetly melodious, as if the feathered creatures of the world in making her their spokesman had loaned her the gift of song.

"I said to myself, 'This is a very great moment. How shall I praise God for letting me be here?' There was only one thing to do. I nestled down in the straw and laid an egg so when it came time for the night's fast to be broken there would be something for hungry folk to eat. And so, ever since that time long ago, an egg has been our way of praise. It is our highest gift."

The rustling in the straw ceased. The

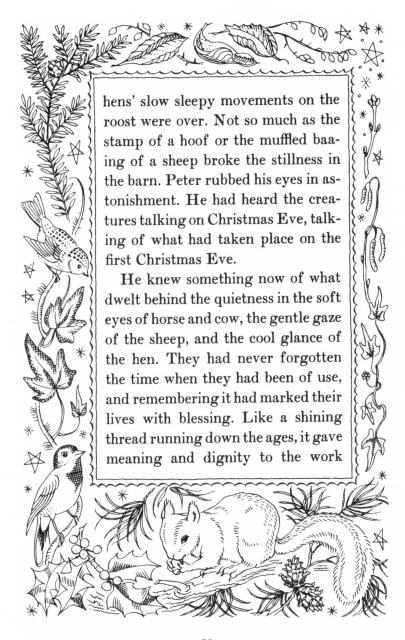

hens' slow sleepy movements on the roost were over. Not so much as the stamp of a hoof or the muffled baaing of a sheep broke the stillness in the barn. Peter rubbed his eyes in astonishment. He had heard the creatures talking on Christmas Eve, talking of what had taken place on the first Christmas Eve.

He knew something now of what dwelt behind the quietness in the soft eyes of horse and cow, the gentle gaze of the sheep, and the cool glance of the hen. They had never forgotten the time when they had been of use, and remembering it had marked their lives with blessing. Like a shining thread running down the ages, it gave meaning and dignity to the work

each one did. Love had made them wise that night, lightening every labor they might do thereafter.

There was a stir among the dark shadows of the barn and Peter saw old Benj coming to stand beside him. It was too dark to see his face, but his form and his footsteps were unmistakable. Peter had thought he was alone in the barn, but it did not surprise him to know that Benj had been there, too.

"I heard them talking together," Peter whispered excitedly. "Did you hear them, Benj—"

"Aye, I heard them," the old man nodded.

"It was wonderful what they said, wasn't it, Benj?"

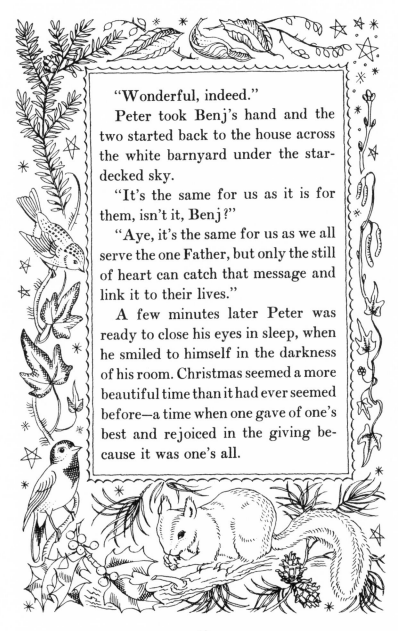

"Wonderful, indeed."

Peter took Benj's hand and the two started back to the house across the white barnyard under the star-decked sky.

"It's the same for us as it is for them, isn't it, Benj?"

"Aye, it's the same for us as we all serve the one Father, but only the still of heart can catch that message and link it to their lives."

A few minutes later Peter was ready to close his eyes in sleep, when he smiled to himself in the darkness of his room. Christmas seemed a more beautiful time than it had ever seemed before—a time when one gave of one's best and rejoiced in the giving because it was one's all.

And then, it was almost as if his mother were standing beside his bed for he could hear her talking to him; but it was not her words, it was the words her mother had used when Martha was a little girl.

"When something wonderful happens to people on Christmas Eve, it is to be cherished in the heart and in the mind. We must not be afraid of the wonderful things, nor must we let others laugh them away from us. Only thus do we learn to hold our dreams—"

Peter smiled to himself again, then he turned his head on his pillow and went to sleep.